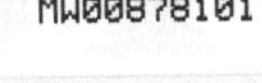

As told by D. P. Sugarborough
Illustrated by Teddy Newton

 **A GOLDEN BOOK • NEW YORK**

 Published in the United States by Golden Books, an imprint of Random House Children's Books, a division of Random House, Inc., 1745 Broadway, New York, NY 10019, and in Canada by Random House of Canada Limited, Toronto, in conjunction with Disney Enterprises, Inc. Golden Books, A Golden Book, A Little Golden Book, the G colophon, and the distinctive gold spine are registered trademarks of Random House, Inc.

www.goldenbooks.com

www.randomhouse.com/kids/disney

Library of Congress Control Number: 2008924750

ISBN: 978-0-7364-2539-1

Printed in the United States of America

10 9 8 7 6 5 4 3 2 1

Presto is a **famous** magician.
He can pull a **rabbit** out of his hat!
With a trick like that, **Presto** gets
everything he could ever want!

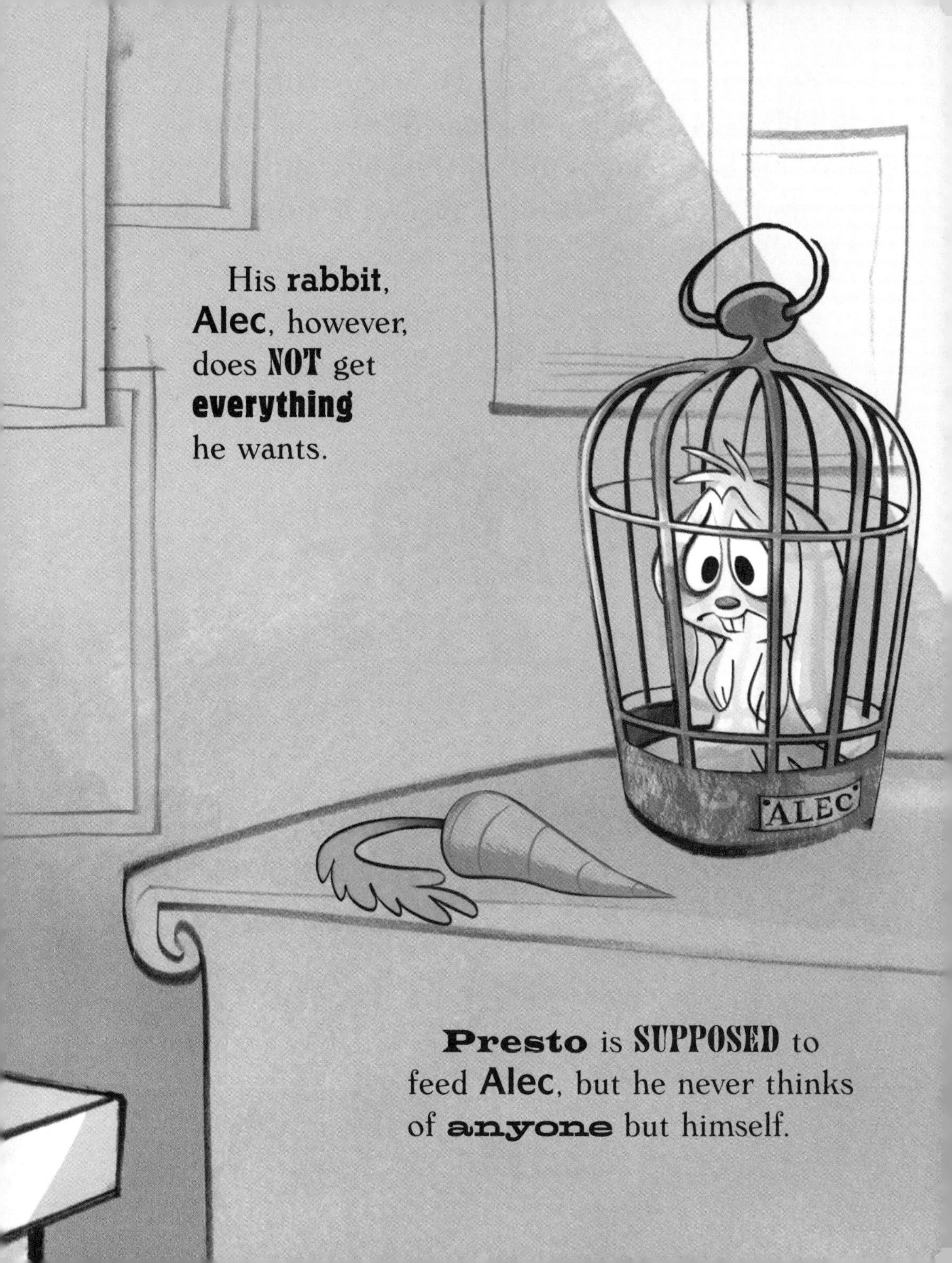

His **rabbit**, **Alec**, however, does **NOT** get **everything** he wants.

Presto is **SUPPOSED** to feed **Alec**, but he never thinks of **anyone** but himself.

Presto likes to practice magic with his two **SPECIAL HATS**. When he reaches through **one** hat, his hand comes **out** of the **other**! **Alec** simply wears the secret **WIZARD** hat, and **Presto** pulls him through the **TOP HAT**!

Practice is done. **Presto** can finally feed **Alec**. Surely there's nothing stopping him now. . . .

Oh, no! The **SHOW** is starting!

Presto leaves Alec
BACKSTAGE (shhh!)
so he can pull him out
ONSTAGE (wink!).

But **Presto** doesn't feel **Alec** in his hat! What could **Alec** possibly be up to?

The poor bunny wants his **carrot**!

But **Presto** wants his **MAGIC** trick!

Alec will
give **Presto**
a trick,
all right.

SNAP!!

Presto teaches **Alec** a lesson!

He **TURNS** the **carrot** into a **flower**!

Now **Alec** teaches **Presto** a lesson!

EERR!
SLAM!!
Yikes!
Alec has Presto's arm!

What will **Alec** make **Presto** do to himself now?

Uh-oh.

What a trick! The crowd cheers. **"Yay!"**

Presto CHASES Alec behind the curtain. As far as he's concerned, tonight's show is over!

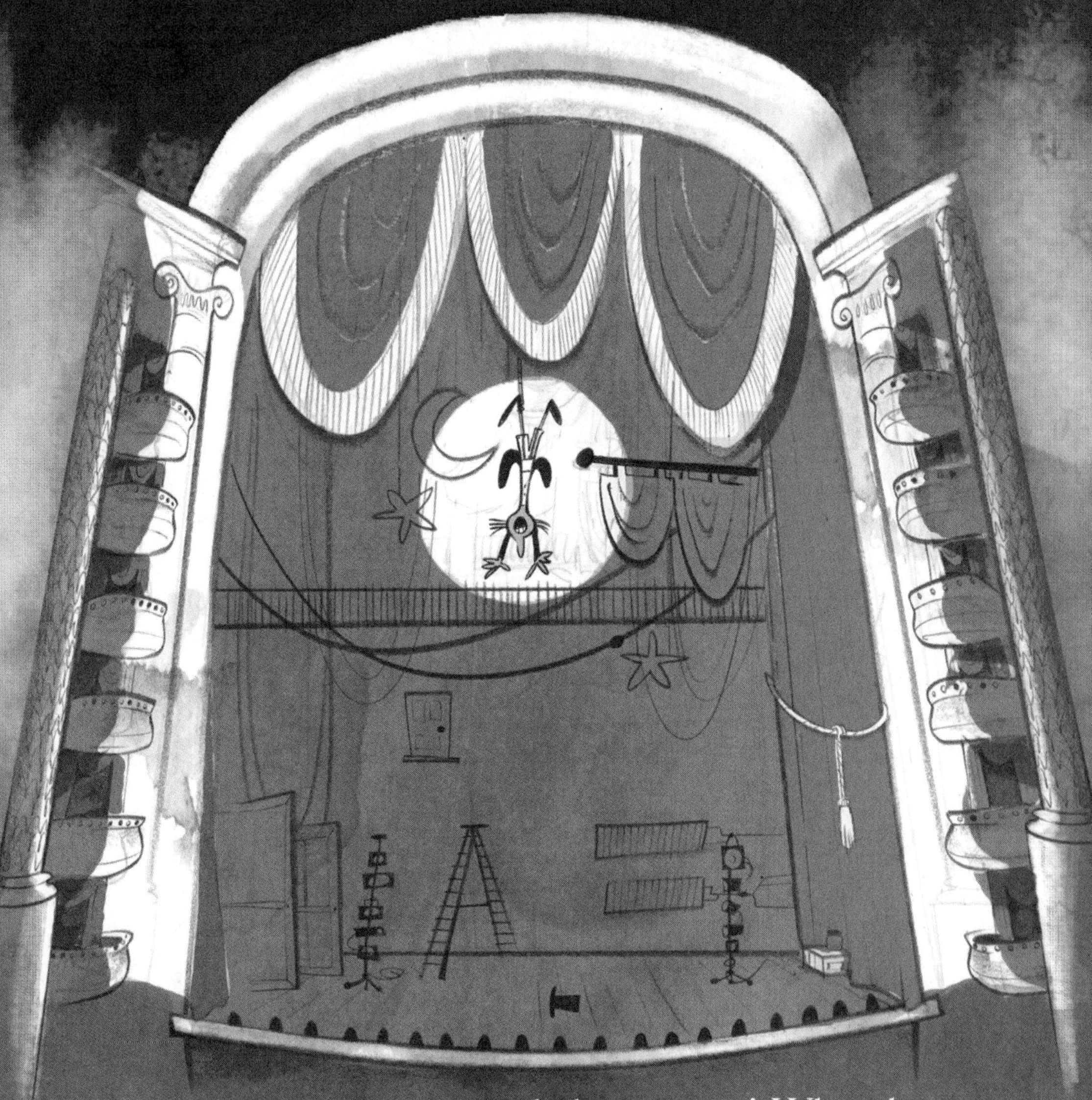

But **Presto** gets tangled in a rope! When he tries to free himself, he accidentally **opens** the curtain, and the rope pulls **Presto** all the way up to the ceiling.

SNAP!!

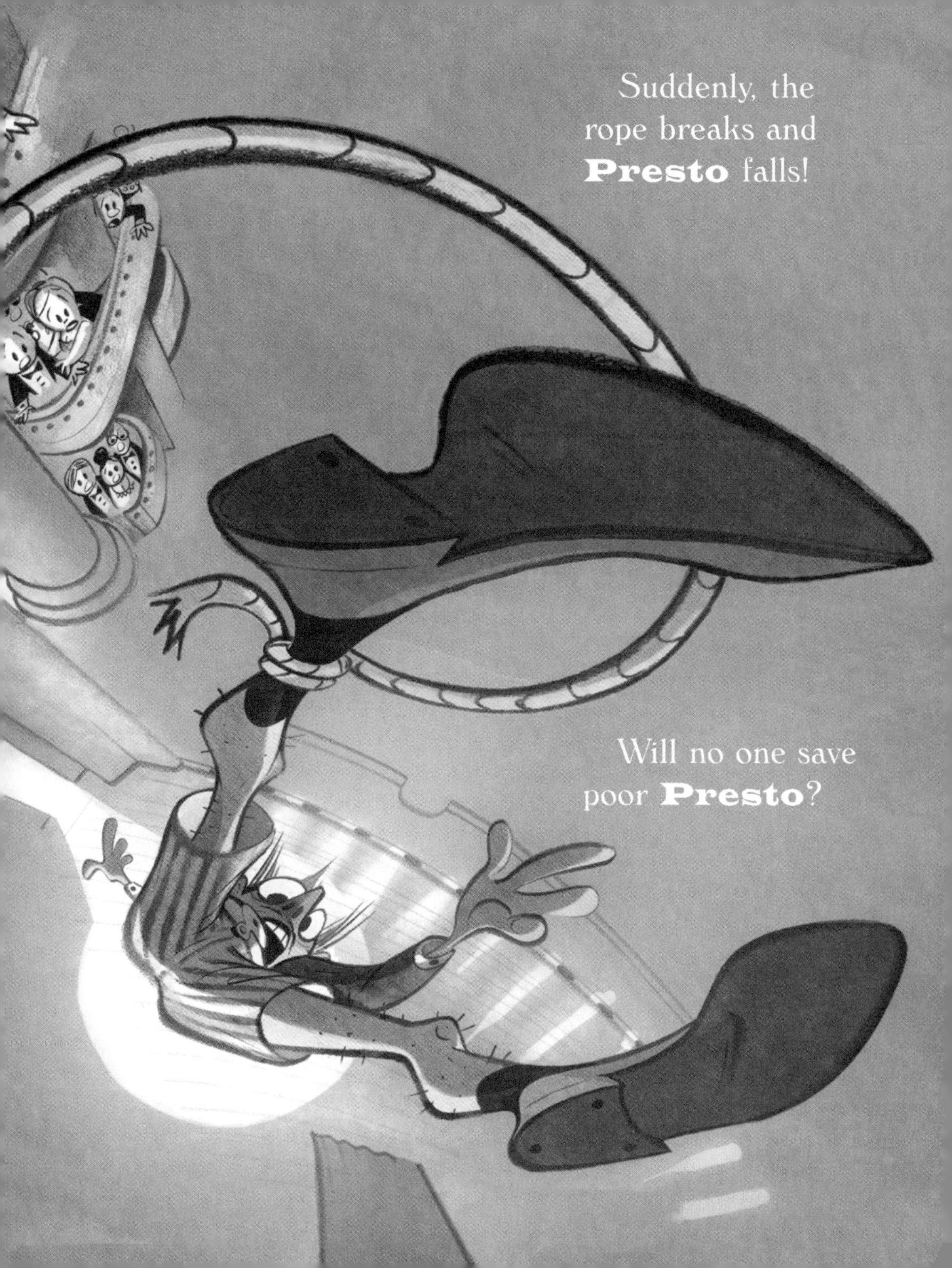

Suddenly, the
rope breaks and
Presto falls!

Will no one save
poor **Presto**?

Alec could just run away. Surely there's nothing stopping him now. . . .

But instead, he places **Presto's** top hat right **under Presto** and . . .

. . . VOILÀ! Presto is SAVED!
The crowd goes Wild! It's the most AMAZING trick they've ever seen! They want more!
ENCORE! ENCORE!

But **Alec** quits!
He and **Presto**
are through!

Presto is
SHOCKED!
Whatever did he do wrong?
Could there be something
his trusty **bunny wants**?

The **CARROT**! **Alec** has taught **Presto** a lesson after all! Now he and **Alec** are a **team**.

THE END
(whew!)